I AM
Bodel

DESIRI OKOBIA

DOV PUBLISHING

This edition published in Great Britain by DOV Publishing
Copyright © 2019 by Desiri Okobia

ISBN: 978-1-9160929-0-7

www.diariesofavisionary.co.uk

Dedications

To all of the children in my life, may you make a positive and lasting impact in your generation.

Hope you enjoy the book.
Much love

—x—

Acknowledgements

I would like to thank my Lord and Saviour Jesus Christ without whom none of this would be possible.

Contents

Foreword

Is your confidence at an all-time low? A healthy level of self-esteem is important in life, especially at work and in our relationships. Traumatic events in life can have a substantial impact on our sense of self-worth and self-esteem. There are issues from our childhood and our family environment that can also take their toll upon our ability to think positively about ourselves. Persistent negative thinking can create a vicious cycle and can leave us feeling even more hopeless and disheartened.

In her book I Am Bodel, Desiri Okobia powerfully deals with insights in the life of her character, a young teenage girl named Bodel. As a teen faced with many obstacles in her life that cause her to go through traumatic experiences, she struggles to deal with situations that arise. Bodel faces everything from low self-esteem to abandonment and bereavement. Eventually Bodel meets a young teenage girl at her school named Rhona, who makes an impact in her life by sharing a powerful revelation with Bodel from her relationship with God. This shared revelation changes Bodel's life forever.

The first time I read this story, it brought tears to my eyes. I believe this book is both timely and necessary for the generation in which we live. I highly recommend that every person, especially young people, read this book—it will change your life forever. Enjoy.

—Pastor Al Lambert
Next Generation Ministries
Potters House Christian Fellowship
London, UK

Chapter 1
Growing Up with Inner Turmoil

Bitterness. It had her bound. Resentment was her rear guard. How could she escape such a grave reality? Everything that she thought was hers was not, and there was nothing she could do about it. Bodel had issues, major issues. She was as insecure as someone standing on a rocky cliff on a windy winter's morning. She was plagued with self-doubt; inadequacy was her partner in crime.

Bodel was a slim girl of above-average height. She possessed a striking beauty that ran deep but only glimmered on the surface. She had the most beautiful brown hair that fell to her lower back. Her skin was naturally tanned, and her eyelashes long and curled. She was a simple beauty, not the overly made-up, highlighted, and blushed beauty that you see in the magazines; she was a subtle, simple soul. Her naturally contoured face was perfectly framed by her tight brown curls, and she had the most striking hazel eyes that glinted in the natural light.

Bodel always wore her hair short—when she was six years old her mother decided to cut it short, and Bodel had never really let it grow back since then.

"Your hair is completely unmanageable," her mother would often complain while struggling to brush through Bodel's tightly curled locks every morning before school. "You're better off cutting it short," she would continue, just before she reached for the scissors.

A slight trim here and there eventually resulted in a huge chop. Bodel would sit with her head buried deep inside her palms, peering through the gaps in her fingers and watching every inch of her glorious waves drop to the floor. Her mother always seemed to feel relieved after hacking away at Bodel's hair. "You look lovely, sweetheart," she would say, with a disturbing half smile.

Her mother wouldn't give a second thought after that, but Bodel would walk upstairs and sob into her pillow. For Bodel, it was more than just a haircut—it was pieces of her self-esteem cascading to the ground like heavy rain. She would look in the mirror and feel disgusted with herself. "I look like a boy," she would complain, repulsed by her own reflection.

Growing up, Bodel always heard her mother's voice ringing in her ears and telling her that her hair was "unmanageable." She got used to cutting it off; every time her hair grew past the nape of her neck, she would cut it short once again. She began to see herself through her mother's eyes—with thick, unmanageable, curly hair that needed to be chopped off at the earliest opportunity.

Bodel grew up with two older brothers, Ted and Jacob. Ted was six years older than Bodel, but Jacob was only a year older than she was. While they were growing up, Bodel was always slightly taller than Jacob; in fact, Bodel was slightly taller than most of the boys in her class. She was often teased during primary school for being so tall and for having short hair.

"There comes that lanky boy," they would say when she walked by, as a mean chorus of giggles filled the air with derision. Bodel didn't say much in response; she got used to ignoring the hurtful comments. Oftentimes she would just allow the words to bounce off the back of her head; she acted like nothing was said.

Jacob tried to defend Bodel whenever he was around, but most of the time he was off playing with his own friends. Bodel spent most of her primary school days isolated and in seclusion. She did manage to make one friend, however, who pretty much stuck by her throughout primary school. Her name was Nina, and she was a sweet girl; she was very popular at school, but she always made time for Bodel. She was the one friend whom Bodel could rely on to save her a seat in the school canteen or involve her in the games during break time on the playground.

Bodel grew up quite introverted and reclusive. She wasn't that confident at making friends because she always feared that people would reject her or make fun of her. Bodel observed the other girls with their pretty, flowery dresses and long hair blowing in the wind and felt inferior in comparison. "They don't like me anyway," she would tell herself as she watched from afar, too afraid to approach the circle of laughter that flowed from the center of the playground.

Bodel found it easier just to keep to herself unless someone came and spoke to her first. Even then, she didn't engage in much conversation. Sometimes it was because of pure nervousness, but other times she felt socially awkward and didn't know what to say. Growing up was difficult for Bodel; she always felt like an outcast, and people's attempts to make her feel included only heightened her sense of insecurity.

When Bodel went on family outings, her parents would buy matching clothes for Ted and Jacob, and she would have to wear an odd, random outfit with some form of princess or pink pattern on it just to show that she was the only girl in the family. If this was meant to make Bodel feel special, then it failed miserably; she felt peculiar. She couldn't really pinpoint why she felt this way. Her brothers were not particularly unpleasant towards her; they didn't make her feel left out at all. In fact, Bodel became a bit of a tomboy, growing up with two older brothers. She went bike riding with them, watched action movies, and played Xbox games, just like her brothers.

One Christmas their father gave Ted and Jacob mountain bikes. Bodel wanted one too, but he gave her a little purple bike with a basket on the front instead. "You can use this bike to ride around gently and carry your shopping," he remarked in an attentive voice that she found both patronizing and belittling.

Bodel didn't need to be reminded that she was a girl; she didn't want to ride around gently and do her shopping. She just wanted to fit in. Bodel wanted to go bike riding with her brothers and come back and talk about how they had courageously conquered the largest mountains, like the action heroes they watched in the films.

Uncertainty plagued her mind; she didn't feel a complete sense of belonging. Her father's sporadic displays of anxiety did not make her feel special; they just made her feel inadequate. Bodel couldn't care less about wearing pink or riding around on a little purple bike; it didn't make any difference to how she felt when she looked in the mirror.

Things took a turn for the worse when Bodel turned seven. Her little sister Rayleigh was born. Rayleigh's hair wasn't unmanageable at all—it was smooth, silky, and straight. Her mother played with Rayleigh's hair like she was a doll, decorating it with bows and precious ribbons. Bodel watched from afar, and when she saw her mother garnishing Rayleigh's hair, she felt crushed by the memory of her fallen curls. She knew that it was wrong for her to be jealous of her new baby sister, but she couldn't help feeling resentful of the quality time that her mother spent with Rayleigh.

"Why didn't Mum take that much time with my hair?"

she thought aloud as she pondered the affectionate display before her. "Why did she give up so easily?"

Bodel knew it was preposterous to feel this way; it was absurd that she was jealous of her little sister. She calculated the absurdity as she tried to shake the feeling of rejection off her shoulders. Bodel had to remind herself that her mother was not doing this on purpose. Her mother cut her hair off because it was unmanageable, not because she didn't love her.

Despite her attempts to shake off all feelings of inadequacy, the whole ordeal with the hair created quite a rift in Bodel's relationship with her mother. She found it easier to relate to her father. They didn't necessarily have to discuss clothing or hair, and Bodel cherished the quality time they spent together when he was home from work. He often took Bodel out for treat nights as a way of celebrating her achievements at school and her commendable behavior. On these treat nights, Bodel would pick a restaurant and her father would treat her to dinner, just her. She normally chose Pizza Hut. It was their special father-daughter time.

When Bodel turned nine, her mother had another baby, Elisa. There were now three daughters in the family. As the years went by and the family grew, the father-daughter dates eventually came to an end. It became too expensive, and Bodel reasoned that her father couldn't take only her out when they had four other children to care for as well. They would all go out for family meals once in a while, but most of the time they ate at home. "Money doesn't grow on trees," her father would remind them when times began to get tough.

When Bodel was ten years old, she was asked to play Joseph in the school's nativity play. She was asked to play Joseph because she was the tallest student in the class; she was even taller than all the boys. Bodel didn't want to play Joseph—she wanted to be Mary.

"I'm a girl; I don't want to play Joseph," she protested to her class teacher, Miss Samuels.

"It doesn't matter, dear. It's only acting," Miss Samuels replied in a most endearing tone that somehow made Bodel feel both at ease and unsettled at the same time. She just wanted to be Mary.

Amy Foster got to play Mary because she was shorter; she had long hair that reached down her back, and she spoke in a soft, projected voice that was fitting for the stage.

Growing up was a tough experience for Bodel. When they took their class photographs at the start of the year, she always had to stand in the back row with the boys, while most of the girls sat on chairs at the front or in a nice, neat row on the floor with their legs crossed. Bodel longed for the day when she would no longer be the odd one out, when all the boys would overtake her in height and the girls would at least catch up with her.

While Bodel sat alone during break time, she would wander off into her own thoughts and imagine herself being someone else and someplace else. Bodel would imagine looking different, speaking different, and being loved by all those around her. Looking in the mirror, however, Bodel saw a tall, slim, flat-chested girl with short hair like a boy's. But she would close her eyes and see a curvy, tanned girl with long, golden-brown curls that reached the lower part of her back. She battled with the conflicting images that flickered between her daydreams and her reality.

As Bodel grew older, she still didn't allow her hair to grow past the nape of her neck, because her mother's crippling words had grabbed hold of her self-esteem. There was a nagging voice in her head that she couldn't shake, a voice reminding her that her hair was "unmanageable." As a result, she kept her hair short for the majority of her school life, at least until she turned fifteen.

Chapter 2
We're Not Your Parents!

Bodel was an outwardly attractive young lady; she just couldn't see it for herself. It was her inner self that was in need of repair; her visage was one of troubling absence. When she entered a room, her very presence filled the atmosphere with uncertainty. A young life once lived to its fullest was now on balancing scales.

"This is the worst day of my life," she cried aloud as she sat in the corner of her crumpled bed sheets, hoping she would wake up from her nightmare.

Moments after the celebration of her fifteenth birthday, Bodel's worst fears had become a reality. The whispering voice that told her she didn't belong, that she didn't fit in, had now taken center stage in her mind. All at once, her worst nightmare had become a daunting truth.

Bodel and her family lived in a terraced house on the outskirts of London. It was a relatively quiet area with not much to do other than take a stroll around the local park. Nothing exciting or seemingly out of the ordinary ever happened to Bodel or her family.

Secondary school was a much more pleasant experience for Bodel than primary school--at least once the bullying and taunting stopped. Her hair was much longer now; it reached midway down her back, and she had filled out her previously slender shape. Bodel had found a way to manage her hair without the assistance of her mother. YouTube taught her everything she needed to know about taming her tight curls. Bodel's best friend, Nina, moved with her to the secondary school that they both wanted to attend, so Bodel found it easy to settle in.

At this point, things were starting to look up for Bodel. She loved school, was an A student, and was a key player on the school netball team. Her favorite subject was art, and her favorite food was pepperoni pizza with a barbecue-sauce base. After Bodel finished school, she wanted to go to college and study interior design. Her dream was to travel the world and create breathtaking interior designs for famous buildings and monuments. That was who she was! She told her parents that once she became a world-famous interior designer, she would fly them over to stay with her in her apartment in Paris. These were her dreams, and she had it all planned out.

One evening Bodel's parents took her out for a birthday treat in a beautiful restaurant overlooking the river Thames. It was just the three of them. This wasn't the usual family birthday routine, so Bodel sensed from the outset that something wasn't quite right. Bodel's parents had told her that they wanted to give her a special birthday treat. Hesitantly Bodel agreed to go, but she was wary of what to expect.

Anxious yet excited, Bodel sat around an elegantly decorated dinner table, scanning the menu from left to right before deciding upon her meal. Bodel's parents didn't say much at dinner that night; there was a constant and overwhelming sense of unease that hung in the atmosphere.

Later that evening, once they returned home, Bodel's parents delivered the news that shattered her whole world into tiny particles of dust. Bodel had just turned fifteen years old, and her parents had decided to let her know that they were not, in fact, her biological parents. They told her that she was adopted! A deep, flustering sensation glued Bodel's insides together as she struggled to take in the news. That evening, Bodel learned that her birth mother had passed away just after she was born; no one mentioned what had happened to her father, so she dared not ask. Bodel kept her inner self locked inside, like a deep wooden chest with a rusted padlock on the outside.

Alone with her tormenting thoughts, Bodel began to replay the conversation over and over again in her mind.

"We just wanted to let you know that your father and I love you very much, Bodel," her mother began with a reassuring voice that sounded both soothing and patronizing at the same time. "There's just something that we have to tell you now, sweetheart," Bodel's mother continued in a slow, soft voice. "You are our daughter and always will be, but we just wanted you to know that . . . we are not actually your biological parents."

Bodel had never been very good at biology, but she got the gist of the conversation by the tone of her mother's voice and the sorrowful look on her father's face.

"What do you mean, biological? You're not really my mum?" she exclaimed with a despairing voice that echoed throughout the house. She turned to her father with a voice of astonishment and said, "So you're not my dad? You're not my parents?"

Resentment swept through her as she screamed aloud in a hysterical fit. A sudden feeling of rejection grabbed hold of her body and shook out all sense of comprehension as she grappled with the realization. Bodel had never felt as alone as she did in that moment.

"Where are my biological parents?" Bodel asked with a trembling voice. She had asked a question for which she was ill-prepared to hear the answer. Then it came, all at once, with a deep and shattering sensation.

"Your birth mother is dead," her adoptive mother began. "She died moments after you were born." The words were spoken but once, but reverberated in a resonating echo in Bodel's ears.

"How can my mother be dead?" Bodel cried with a faint, fearful voice. And just like that, abandonment reared its ugly head like a voiceless serpent and spewed its poison within the young girl's mind.

"So did you collect me from the hospital then?" Bodel continued with a childish ignorance. "Did you know my mother?" Bodel's line of inquiry was focused entirely on her mother, as no one had mentioned her father.

It was then that Bodel's adoptive mother, Maddie, explained to Bodel that her birth mother had been a close friend of hers. She had been told that she might have complications during childbirth, and the two women had agreed that if anything happened to her, Maddie would adopt the child and raise it as her very own. When the unfortunate ordeal took place, Maddie kept her word and adopted Bodel to raise as her own child. Maddie was no stranger to the world of parenting, as she already had two sons of her own before Bodel was born; so she and her husband, Luis, agreed to adopt Bodel and raise her as part of the family. They decided that once Bodel was fifteen years old, they would tell her the truth about her birth mother.

Early on a breezy winter morning, Bodel sat huddled in the corner of her half-made bed. Brushing her hair in slow motion, she gazed longingly out her bedroom window, wishing she could be somewhere else. The wind struck forcibly against her window; the trees swayed in a circular motion, and the sky was a darker shade of gray than usual.

"I often sit and wonder what it would be like to be somebody else," Bodel whispered aloud to herself. Longingly she stared out her bedroom window. She pondered the vast field of greenery that surrounded her otherwise dull and secluded life.

Bodel wanted so much out of life, but everything seemed so far from her reach. She was only fifteen, but she had lived a life beyond her years. She had grown up among a family of strangers, or so it felt to Bodel.

"Being adopted isn't the worst thing that can happen to a young girl," Bodel thought aloud as she wandered aimlessly around her room before drawing together her perfectly frilled curtains.

"Fifteen years, fifteen years!" Bodel repeated, as she sat sobbing in a pool of self-pity. She just couldn't fathom the idea that she had grown up in a home for fifteen years only to find out that the woman she thought was her mother was just a stranger—a stranger who had taken her in as a baby.

"Is this love, or is this deception?" she asked herself thoughtfully, as she silently examined every memory that had ever graced her downtrodden heart.

The recent disclosure had left Bodel desperate and disheartened—she felt as though she was caught between a rock and a hard place. On the one hand, she was grateful that she had grown up in such a warm, loving, and caring family. But on the other hand, there was another thought that she couldn't shake off no matter how hard she tried. It continued to linger on the inside of her already-exposed heart: why hadn't her biological father ever tried to contact her? Did he even know that she existed? These questions consumed her mind until the minutes turned to hours and the hours turned to days.

Bodel wore her heart on her sleeve. There was no hiding it—everyone could see that she was going through an ordeal, a whirlwind of emotions that couldn't be tamed. She was a wreck, a glass jar of shattered emotions, desperately searching for a sense of belonging. She no longer felt that she belonged in the home where she had grown up—the only home she had ever known.

"My mother isn't my mother," she murmured aloud, as she sat scribbling away in her hardback journal and trying to make sense of what was left of her broken identity.

"Bodel! Bodel!" the woman downstairs yelled. This was Bodel's adoptive mother, Maddie, the woman that Bodel had once called "Mum" with a sense of pride and serenity that had soothed her very soul. That serenity was gone now. It seemed somewhat futile to impart such a sentiment upon a willing stranger, Bodel reasoned.

"It's time for school," Maddie continued.

"I'm not feeling too good today," Bodel replied with a slight hesitation in her voice, hoping that Aunt Maddie (as she now decided to call her) would cease to persist with this unreasonable line of orders. Bodel didn't want to go to school; she didn't want to go anywhere. She just wanted to sit in her room alone, trying to make sense of the mess that had once been her perfectly ordered life.

Something unnerving had taken place inside Bodel since that birthday evening following the restaurant meal. Bodel didn't feel as though she belonged in her home anymore, and she didn't even feel as though she could refer to her parents as "Mum" and "Dad."

While Bodel was growing up, she had been taught that she was not to call adults by their first names; instead, she was to refer to them as "aunt" and "uncle," as this was seen as a sign of respect. As Bodel began to feel uncomfortable within her home, it affected the very core of her being and the way that she viewed life. Eventually she began to refer to her adoptive parents as "Aunt Maddie" and "Uncle Luis."

"You've been off school for almost two weeks," Aunt Maddie persisted. "They'll be sending the education officer down here if we're not careful," she continued with a slight snigger, partly hoping that the light humor would persuade Bodel to see reason.

The way Bodel's mind was set at that moment, however, there was no reasoning with her. There was no sense of rationality and no open door through which to persuade her to move. She just wanted to sit alone, pondering and escaping into her thoughts. She was happy in her own world; things were safe there. And so she sat, motionless and content in the center of her life's wreckage, drifting into a deep sea of recollections. Her mind took her to a place of contentment where she could pretend that none of this had happened.

This time last week, Bodel had known exactly who she was—Bodel Pascoe, daughter of Luis and Maddison Pascoe. She was fifteen years old, had two older brothers, and two younger sisters. She had not always been happy, but at least she had been content. Despite being adopted, Bodel had never purposely been made to feel like the odd one out in her family home; she was loved and cared for and protected like any other child of her age. The only thing was that she didn't look like anyone else in her family, and whenever she went on family outings, people often commented on the fact that she looked so different from her siblings. They didn't comment in a cruel, nasty way that made Bodel feel uneasy, but rather in the most endearing of tones.

Bodel always took as a compliment their comments on her beautiful golden-brown curls and her naturally tanned skin. She was darker than anyone else in her family.

Aunt Maddie was a pretty and petite woman. She had straight, dark-black hair, pale skin, and a small cute face with perfectly formed high cheekbones that reached her ears when she smiled. Her eyes were almond shaped; they were deeply mysterious and a piercing, glistening green color. Aunt Maddie's other daughters, Rayleigh and Elisa, were her spitting image. Bodel was her polar opposite, but that hadn't bothered Bodel at all. Things only started to go downhill when Aunt Maddie decided to break the news to Bodel that she was not, in fact, her real mother. Aunt Maddie had always said that she would tell Bodel the truth when she was old enough to understand. It's not that Bodel couldn't understand what adoption was, but Aunt Maddie just didn't feel that there was ever a right time to turn a person's world upside down in such an excruciating manner.

There was still a suspicious and niggling part of Bodel's brain that didn't really believe her birth mother was gone, but there was another part of her brain in which she blamed herself. Bodel concluded with a childlike innocence that if her mother had passed away just after she was born, then she must have been the cause of her death.

The reality was that there was nothing anyone could have done to prevent what had happened. Bodel's mother had died after childbirth; there were complications outside of anyone's control. As rational as it sounded and as obvious as it was, Bodel still could not rid herself of the niggling sensation that she was somehow to blame for this unfortunate turn of events.

The strange thing is, Bodel never really grieved the loss of her mother. Even after she found out, she kept her feelings bottled up inside. She kept her feelings inside, as though in breakable glass like an old, familiar milk bottle. Her inner turmoil, however, was easy to perceive, and if she were pushed over a certain limit, she could quite easily crack and shatter into thousands of small pieces. Bodel did not want to grieve because she didn't want to seem ungrateful towards Uncle Luis and Aunt Maddie for all that they had done for her. She told herself that if she grieved, then she was somehow showing them that she did not want to be part of their family.

That day, Bodel left the family meeting with a forced smile and a whirlwind of unanswered questions that plagued her for weeks. If she had kept talking, she would have upset herself even more, or so she thought. She would have been digging for answers that no one could give her. She now found herself searching to no avail to fill the large, empty hole that had formed within her heart.

As the hours turned to days, and the days turned to weeks, Bodel was not deceiving anyone with her erratic displays of courage. Bodel desperately wanted to pretend that she was fine. She reasoned that if she could convince everyone around her that she was coping well, then that would subsequently ease the pain that she was trying so hard to suppress. Bodel had mastered the art of self-deception; she had learned how to put up a brave face while struggling to hold herself together. On the inside, though, she was an emotional wreck.

Bodel felt that there were too many questions left unanswered; there was just too much that she didn't know. If the death of her mother was something that Bodel could not control, then she would have to make sure she controlled every other aspect of her life. With that, Bodel became a control freak—she wanted to make sure everything that she could keep within her reach was kept within her reach. She found herself doing strange things like waking up in the middle of the night to check that her closed bedroom windows were still closed. Bodel behaved like this because she did not want any more surprises; she didn't want anyone else to be able to drop a bombshell of destruction upon her and tell her that there was "nothing she could do about it."

Sometimes in life, people go through things that shake them into a state of insecurity and paranoia. They find themselves doing things that they never thought they would do. In Bodel's mind, she was just trying to secure herself; she wanted to regain a sense of control. To everyone else, however, her behavior was just strange. She checked closed windows to make sure nobody had opened them while she was sleeping. She checked empty pockets in her jeans to make sure nobody had put anything in them. Before she sat on a chair, she would run her fingers up and down the legs to make sure that they were sturdy and she wouldn't fall off. Bodel had been nothing like that before she found out about her mother, but it was her own unique way of grieving. It was unfortunate, however, that it sometimes manifested itself in gripping outbursts of paranoia that blurred her line of reasoning.

Bodel managed to get almost two weeks off from school so she could process this information and then rediscover herself. She was hoping to gain another week in which she could rationalize this material and prepare herself to control her surroundings at school as well. The strangest thing of all was that all the while Bodel was off from school, she did not shed one tear of grievance.

Chapter 3
Back to School

"It's eight o'clock in the morning and I'm still here," Bodel concluded as she sat scrunched up in the corner of her cluttered room, gazing through the window at a cat that had stumbled its way into the fenced-off garden. It was a ginger cat, a golden-brown color, with sharp, pointy whiskers stemming from its perfectly contoured cheeks. Cats often wandered in and out of Bodel's family garden; she remembered this as she sat studying the cat and scrutinizing its every move, like a private investigator. The cat continued to wander waywardly across the lawn without a care in the world.

"Where is its owner?" Bodel wondered as she sat slowly sipping her chocolate-flavored milk covered with marshmallows, desperately trying to escape to cheerier, happier times. There was something about warm, chocolate-flavored milk that reminded Bodel of the early days of her childhood when everything was simple and basic, like a white cotton bathrobe.

"When did life get so complicated?" she whimpered aloud, searching for an avenue to release the pain that was bubbling up inside her. As she shrieked aloud, the cat on the lawn became suddenly alert and darted into the neighboring garden. And there Bodel sat, once again preoccupied with her pondering, wandering mind.

"Bodel!" wailed the woman downstairs in a voice full of tension. "It's time to go, or you are going to be late."

At that moment, Bodel's heart jumped into her throat. She couldn't care less about being late; in fact, she didn't want to go to school at all. School was the last place on earth that she wanted to be. All of a sudden, Bodel's thoughts gathered in her and shook her back to reality. She knew that there were no more excuses, no more procrastination; it was time to go. She had to pluck up enough courage to face the world once again. It was time to take that long, winding walk back through the echoing iron gates where life begins.

Bodel stood up with obedience and a false sense of confidence that deceived everybody but herself. Dressed from head to toe in garments that were designed to ensure that she felt a sense of belonging, she picked up her perfectly bound notebook and trudged towards her bedroom door. "Wearing this uniform won't make any difference," Bodel convinced herself. "I won't fit in there anymore. I don't fit in anywhere," she told herself repeatedly.

Dragging herself across her room, her mind filled with discouraging thoughts, Bodel took one last gaze at her reflection in the rectangular-shaped, wardrobe-door mirror. She paused for a moment to gloss over the sides of her cheekbones with a layer of purple glitter that sparkled under the light. She gave herself a sweet pep talk and headed reluctantly towards the front door.

Bodel sat in her mother's car, still as a statue. Angst, anxiety, and apprehension had grabbed and consumed the most agile parts of her brain. She no longer remembered the friends she once had, the lessons in which she had previously excelled, and the sports she had loved to play. As far as Bodel was concerned, she was an outsider now. No one understood her.

"I'll be back to pick you up at three thirty, sweetheart," said Aunt Maddie with an apprehension that Bodel had never heard before.

The walk from the car to the gates was the shortest part of the journey to school, but for Bodel, the school gates seemed miles away from the car. Bodel prepared herself for the worst; she imagined all the questions that would be thrown at her about why she had been away from school for so long. She had already constructed a full-blown scenario in her mind about the gossiping, the rumors, and the misconceptions. She dreaded the thought of being mocked, ridiculed, and interrogated like a criminal in a courtroom. Troubling thoughts plagued her as she prepared for that long, excruciating walk towards the gigantic iron gates otherwise known as "school."

She got out of the car and began to walk grudgingly towards the gates, accompanied by an aura of uncertainty and the whisper of rejection that nibbled away at her insides. Full of trepidation, she paused for a moment and looked back at Aunt Maddie. "Will they look at me differently?" she asked.

"Of course not, sweetheart. You'll be absolutely fine," Aunt Maddie replied, giving a warm smile as she pulled away from the curb.

"Everyone must know what happened to me; they must be having a right old chuckle at my expense." The voice in her head droned on with a sniggering, mocking tone.

Her thoughts were loud, extremely loud. They were almost too loud to silence, and they drowned out every other voice in Bodel's immediate surroundings. As Bodel began to walk towards the school building, a wave of chittering and chattering began to fill her ears. The rest of the latecomers were hurrying in closely behind her, trying to make it inside the building before the second bell. The wind was still whistling its way through the bare, leafless trees, and the clouds were hidden amidst the light-gray blanket that was the sky. It was a calm day with only a hint of impending rain.

There Bodel stood—in front of the iron gates, in the midst of chaos, surrounded by confusion, grappling with insecurity. She was secretly hoping for a time when she would just wake up from her nightmare and return to a state of normality.

"Bye, Mum!" she bellowed from the corner of the pavement. Bodel wanted to make sure that everyone heard her display of endearment and knew that she belonged to someone, that she came from a "normal" home. There was one part of her that wanted desperately to pretend that she was her usual smart, accomplished self, but an even larger part of her that only wanted the troubling voices to cease and clear the space within her mind. She didn't want to be frightened and fearful anymore. She didn't want to wake up wrestling with a misplaced sense of belonging and self-worth for a moment longer. With that, Bodel began her brave stroll beyond the iron gates and back to the conservatory institution otherwise known as school.

Chapter 4
Living a Lie

At morning registration time, Bodel normally sat in the center of the classroom. When the opportunity arose, she would leave her seat and scramble her way to the back so she could have a good old catch-up with her best friend, Nina.

Nina was a popular girl at secondary school. She had the most beautiful kinky brown hair that was tightly braided and reached to the lower part of her back. Her eyes were a lighter shade of brown than usual, and everyone absolutely adored her. What's more, Nina came from a "normal" home, or so Bodel perceived. She lived with her mum, dad, two brothers, and a new baby sister. Bodel had thought she came from a normal home too. She had a father, a mother, two brothers, and two sisters—only to recently discover that they were not actually her real family; her real mother had been dead for fifteen years.

Lining up outside the classroom was overwhelming for Bodel. The questions, the looks, the stares, and the explanations that she wished she had all filled her with a deep sense of anguish. Bodel thought that she had prepared herself for questions, but can a person ever really be prepared to let everyone know that their whole life has been a lie? She was a fabricator, she concluded. The embarrassment, the humiliation, the questions she couldn't answer, and the repercussions were endless.

Bodel was not prepared for this moment. She didn't even know where to start, so she decided to keep her interactions both short and superficial. Bodel rationalized within her mind that if she could manage to be in the presence of Nina without letting on that her whole life had collapsed before her very eyes, she could get through just about anything.

"Hi, Bodz!" Nina screamed with an excitement that seemed almost sarcastic. Well, at least that's how Bodel perceived it to be. "How have you been? I tried calling you, but your mum said that you were really ill," Nina continued with a genuine sense of compassion that Bodel perceived to be a subtle attempt at digging for more information.

At that moment, Bodel was caught between a rock and a hard place. It was a make-or- break moment. It was Groundhog Day— she had seen this moment before. All of a sudden, a whirlwind of emotions began to take control of the better part of her senses; she found words pouring out of her mouth like a floodgate.

"Yes, I have been extremely unwell recently, so I begged my mum to let me stay at home as I didn't want to be in school with such a terrible flu virus. I was worried that it might be contagious." Bodel began to entangle herself in a web of dishonesty.

"I did call you, but your mum said you weren't taking any calls," Nina continued. "You even missed Ariella's birthday party on Saturday. Must have been one serious flu," Nina replied in slight jest.

"Oh, really? How was the party?" Bodel pretended to be interested.

Bodel had begun her tale of falsehoods and didn't think it possible to stop. Anything was better than telling the story of how she no longer had parents, a family, or any real identity. Anything was better than exposing the fact that she had been deceived, dumbfounded, and flabbergasted by this sudden realization that she did not actually have a real mother or somewhere that she felt comfortable to call her home. Bodel cut the conversation short and proceeded to her seat in the center of the classroom, where she sat with her head buried inside a Charles Dickens novel, hoping that this would be the end of the interrogation.

"I just have to get through today and keep smiling," she told herself, hoping no one would sense the aura of discontentment that projected itself from the innermost part of her being. Bodel continued throughout her day with head down, mouth frozen in a grin, and a heart full of fragmented emotions.

Chapter 5
Rebellious Ways

Bodel walked into her English lesson and sat in the wrong seat on purpose. She decided that today was going to be one of those days; she didn't want to play by the rules. Everyone always expected Bodel to sit down at the front of the class, participate in the lesson, and complete her work. People didn't know how troubled and disturbed she really was. She had become used to pretending, but on this day, she started acting out of character, almost like a passive cry for help. Sitting at the back of the class, giggling with the student next to her, Bodel waited for her teacher to notice her.

Miss Morelli always put the class into specific seats. She knew exactly where everyone was meant to be sitting, and she could tell just by scanning the room if someone was out of place.

"Bodel, can you go back to your seat please?" Miss Morelli asked, in a polite tone at first.

Bodel sat staring at her teacher's face, partially in a daydream and partially in a deliberate state of rebellion.

"I want to sit here today," Bodel said.

"You need to stay in your own seat unless you have permission to move," Miss Morelli repeated.

"But I can't see from there," Bodel added.

Astonished at this display of disobedience, Miss Morelli repeated her instruction once more in an increasingly frustrated tone. "Bodel Pascoe, you are holding up the lesson. Please move back to your seat!"

All eyes were on Bodel by now. This was completely out of character for her. She wasn't used to being in this position, but it felt good to be the center of attention for once. There was no reason for it, but the childlike rebel inside of her was so thrilled with basking in the overflow of attention that she just sat there in stubbornness.

"I can't see from the front," she repeated in an obstinate tone.

Miss Morelli was more shocked than anything else; she couldn't quite understand what had gotten into Bodel or why she had decided to create this scene at the start of her English lesson. Bodel couldn't work it out either. She loved English, but she was tired of always being looked at as Bodel Pascoe—the straight-A student who didn't have a care in the world. In reality, she was distraught and troubled inside.

There were some students in her class who were often taken out of regular lessons to talk to the school counselor. Bodel wasn't one of them, but she wanted something. She wanted someone to take the time to listen to her struggles—but at the same time she didn't. Her pride held her back.

Desperately Bodel wanted to cover up her distress, but it began to manifest itself in bizarre ways. Bodel dashed her books to the floor, buried her head on the table, and obstinately refused to go back to her seat. Her frantic cry for attention came to a halt when the vice principal was called to the classroom. He just so happened to be on behavior duty that day.

Fear took hold of Bodel as she was summoned from the doorway by the vice principal. The vice principal, Mr. Rowlson, was an energetic man. He paced up and down the hallways like a patrol officer, checking uniforms, making sure student planners were on desks, and ensuring that the school rules were strictly complicd with at all times. Being led down the hallway by the vice principal was not how Bodel had expected her first day back at school to end. One bad decision had quickly spiraled out of control.

"Why were you sitting in the wrong seat, Bodel?" Mr. Rowlson asked with a stern look on his face, refusing to blink. "You were asked to move on numerous occasions, yet you refused to comply," he continued.

Bodel had no defense. She didn't reply at first; instead, she bowed her head in humiliation. She didn't repeat her comment about not being able to see from the back. She just said, "I don't know what I was thinking." Bodel didn't have the energy to say anything else.

Mr. Rowlson spoke in a daunting tone accompanied by an unsympathetic gaze, and Bodel did not want to dig a deeper hole than she had already dug. The smart comments evaporated from Bodel's mouth, and at this moment, her throat tightened. Apprehension had taken its toll. All she could think about was the reaction on the faces of Uncle Luis and Aunt Maddie once they learned that Bodel had been called out of class by the vice principal for "persistently defiant behavior."

Mr. Rowlson scribbled her name down on a yellow detention slip and handed Bodel a copy before ushering her back to the classroom. "She'll go back to her seat now," he reassured Miss Morelli, as he stuck his head into the doorway of the classroom.

Bodel moved back to her seat, embarrassed by the unnecessary ordeal that had just taken place.

Chapter 6
Being the Odd One Out

Sitting solemnly in a corner of the overcrowded lunch hall, Bodel stared out the window. She took one painstakingly deep breath as she managed to gulp down the last part of her enormous glass of tap water. She was in urgent need of nourishment, but she had lost her appetite for everything but warm chocolate milk.

Bodel couldn't let anyone know what she was really going through, or so she thought. Instead, she disguised her plate to look like that of a healthy fifteen-year-old girl with an appetite for life. Her half-full plate was nicely decorated with a small side of battered fish, freshly cut chips, and perfectly rounded garden peas.

Lunchtime was usually the best part of the school day. It was the time to catch up on the events of the morning and start the countdown to home time. However, once again Bodel attempted to escape from her current surroundings and drifted off into her own dreamland. She sat alone, staring gloomily out the canteen window and looking expectantly at the white puffs of smoke-like clouds that drifted through the air. They were a transparent type of white, almost fading into gray. The clouds seemed to travel in packs, gliding slowly through the sapphire sky, motioning themselves from the east to the west and then disappearing into a pile of nothingness.

There was one particular cloud that caught Bodel's attention. It was a large puffy, grayish-looking cloud, and it stood out amongst the other white cotton balls. As Bodel sat staring at that gray cloud, her eyes began to well up with tears—it became almost unbearable. She was suddenly overwhelmed by a feeling of isolation that she couldn't shake. Her eyes welled up as she fixed her gaze on the gray cloud. It didn't seem as if rain was anywhere in sight, and the gray cloud continued to float camouflaged amongst the rest. Bodel was fascinated by the gray cloud; she didn't even acknowledge the rest of the beautiful scenery within her visual field as she pondered.

Then it came—a teardrop fell from the inner corner of one of her beautiful, almond-shaped eyes and created a minuscule puddle on the oak surface of the rectangular-shaped canteen table. Bodel swiftly averted her gaze and reached for a crumpled piece of tissue in her blazer pocket so as to wipe the impending tears from her face. She couldn't let anyone know that she was about to sob and whimper like a baby. A sudden, ridiculous feeling of humiliation came over Bodel as she wiped every trace of weakness from the corners of her eyes.

"Am I like the gray cloud?" she wondered to herself. "It floats so gracefully amongst its pure-white counterparts and still leaves its unique print on the sapphire sea in the sky. All of the clouds eventually evaporate anyway," Bodel reasoned in her heart, "so what does it matter whether they are white or gray?"

Little did Bodel know that the gray cloud was not the odd one out; it had a unique purpose of its very own. The cloud was not an off-white color. In fact, it was a perfectly fashioned gray painted by its Creator—a lighter shade of gray, just gray enough to carry the fruits of the coming season. Bodel closed her eyes for a moment in order to hold back the impending tears. When she glanced back up at the sapphire-blue sky, all the clouds had evaporated into the west and the sky was clear again.

All of a sudden, a loud ringing sound woke Bodel up from her daydream; it was time for her final lesson of the day. "We've got double PE," said Nina excitedly, as she picked up her empty plate.

Bodel's plate was still half-full. She had managed to pick at her garden peas between her gulps of water, but that was about it. "Oh no, I didn't even get to finish my lunch," she wailed with a fabricated sense of disappointment that once again deceived everybody but herself.

"What were you doing all this time?" Nina asked, as if Bodel had not been sitting right next to her the whole time and staring out the window.

Sometimes people ask questions that they know the answer to just to avoid the overbearing awkwardness that exists between two people when it is obvious that something isn't right. Nina knew that something wasn't right with Bodel. She had been out of school for over a week, and now she had come back with no appetite for life and no real explanation. Nina did not buy into Bodel's contagious flu story, not for one minute. Although Nina was fully aware that something wasn't right with Bodel, there was nothing she could do at this point. Nina rested in the knowledge that if Bodel didn't want to open up and tell her what was really going on, she just had to be patient and hope that everything would work out for her. It's hard being fifteen.

"I was just thinking about something; got a lot on my mind, that's all," Bodel replied with a half smile, as she picked up her rucksack from the chair to her left.

As usual, Bodel got up and inspected the legs of the chair she was sitting on to make sure they were still strong and sturdy and the next person that sat there didn't fall off. Nina looked at

Bodel with an expression of concern. She hid her concerns behind an uneasy, smiling face as they walked arm in arm out of the canteen.

"Let's go, Bodel. We don't want to be late for PE. Miss Dobson gives out detentions for fun," Nina remarked in a lighthearted fashion. They scurried out of the canteen and headed off to the final lesson of the day.

Chapter 7
Outbursts of Rage

PE was different today. After changing into their PE kits, the class gathered inside the sports hall as usual. They were then introduced to a visiting teacher who wanted to teach the kids how to do rock climbing. At this point, the class was separated into small groups. The girls on the netball team were taken outside to a different part of the playground. Nina wasn't on the netball team, so she stayed with the rock-climbing group, while Bodel went outside.

It was freezing cold out on the netball courts, and Miss Dobson was giving the team a pep talk before PE started.

"Year 10, as you all know, we have a match next week against Hertford Grammar," she began. "I'm not worried about you girls because you did great last time. We are one game away from getting to the finals."

The netball team was playing in an interschool league. Bodel had missed the last game while she was off for the past couple of weeks, but she was keen to get back on the court. Miss Dobson was an athletic woman, although much fuller than the average netball coach. She had short blonde hair tied back into a ponytail, and she spoke with a calm, authoritative voice. Bodel got along well with Miss Dobson; she was different from all the other teachers. She didn't seem to fit into any particular mold; she was just herself. Her enthusiasm for her subject entered the room long before she did. Her passion for teamwork was contagious, and it added a pleasant feeling of solidarity to the atmosphere.

"Welcome back," she said to Bodel with a warm and endearing smile. "We missed you at the game last week."

"Thanks, Miss. Glad to be back." Bodel was happy. She liked being on the netball team because it gave her a sense of belonging; she felt that she was needed, a crucial member of the team.

Bodel normally played goal attack on the team. There was another girl on the team, Tia, who was much taller than Bodel. In fact, Tia was the tallest girl on the team. Bodel knew too well what that felt like. Tia was supposed to play the goal shooter; that was her position, but she always caused a commotion when it was time to take positions.

"I want to play goal attack," Tia would demand. Miss Dobson had asked her to play the goal shooter because of her height; she was thinking about what was best for the team. Tia, however, wanted to be able to run around the court. "I don't want to stay in the semicircle and shoot," she would complain.

Eventually Miss Dobson agreed that they—Tia and Bodel—could swap positions halfway through the game.

Bodel didn't really get along with Tia. It wasn't just because of her behavior on the netball courts; it was just her general tendency to try to control people. Tia was the bossy girl that everyone followed around; she was the leader of the pack. Bodel was too quiet for Tia.

"Bodel is so boring," Tia would say, "the way she just stands there and doesn't say anything."

Bodel didn't have much to say to Tia, and she couldn't be bothered to deal with her tantrums, even on a normal day. She usually just smiled and pretended that she didn't hear Tia's pathetic cries for affirmation. Bodel was not interested in following her around the school and stroking her self-image. That may have caused a slight bruise to Tia's ego, but Bodel was just not interested. She would much rather keep herself to herself; popularity was not that high on her list of priorities.

As a result, Tia sometimes made snide remarks about Bodel, either in front of her face or behind her back. Bodel didn't care at all; she had gotten so used to ignoring negativity in her early years of childhood that this did not faze her in the slightest. Bodel fully understood the root of Tia's frustrations, so she allowed the comments to drop to the ground like water off a duck's back.

The game started. They were practicing against a visiting team in preparation for the game that was to take place the following week. When it was time to take positions, Tia took Bodel's bib, as usual, so Bodel put on the goal-shooter bib and went to stand in her place. When halftime came, the girls were down by three points. It was time to switch positions as agreed, but then Tia came along. "I'm keeping my position," she said as she walked away from the team huddle.

Bodel stared in astonishment. Miss Dobson was standing on the other side of the playground, speaking to the teacher from the other school. Anger rushed through Bodel's veins as she watched Tia trotting off across the court as if her word on the matter was final. She was reminded of all the other times that Tia had attempted to belittle her and dismiss her presence.

"We were supposed to swap at halftime," Bodel blurted out with an aggression that she had never demonstrated before.

"I'm keeping my position," Tia repeated. It was the word my that hit a nerve for Bodel. Tia knew full well that it was not her position at all. Miss Dobson allowed them to swap at halftime only because Tia had complained. Bodel had not said anything about that because she understood what it was like to be placed in a particular role because of your height. But this time, Tia had overstepped the mark. She was dismissive and obnoxious, refusing to swap positions for no apparent reason.

Fury came over Bodel suddenly, and she couldn't control it. She closed her eyes; she saw red; she couldn't shake it off. Bodel was enraged—filled with a furious rage she had never before experienced. She ran straight up to Tia and slapped her in the face. She grabbed her by the collar and threw her to the ground. She kicked Tia numerous times and punched the smug look right off her domineering face. Years of built-up anger and resentment were released that day. Bodel felt relieved, and for a moment, she was filled with a satisfying sense of release. Surprisingly, no one had come over to break up the beatdown. Then a loud whistle woke Bodel out of her daydream. It was time to go back for the second half of the game.

Bodel paused for a minute and then realized that besides the battle that had just taken place within her mind, nothing had changed. She had not actually grabbed Tia by the collar and thrown her to the ground; she had not recovered the position that was rightfully hers. Much to her relief, she had not lashed out and caused a catastrophe in the middle of the netball court.

Bodel stood still on the corner of the netball court, just outside the team huddle, still filled with years of infuriation, anger, and resentment for which she couldn't find an avenue of relief. Was she really that angry at Tia for not swapping bibs? Did she really want to go to the place that her mind had taken her in that moment? Was that the real source or solution to her fury?

Let's face it—brutally lashing out at an annoying girl on the netball court was not going to begin to solve Bodel's deep-rooted issues. Abandonment, low self-esteem, and a misguided sense of worth were the things that Bodel battled on a daily basis. No one knew where Bodel's mind had just gone, because she internalized it so well. All people saw was Tia sauntering around the court and Bodel standing still, quiet as a mouse. Nothing had changed. Her eyes had not turned red, her body had not swelled up with heat, and she wasn't going to jump on Tia and pull her hair out as she had just imagined herself doing. Instead, she bowed her head, took off her netball bib, and walked off the court. She didn't know where she was going, but she knew she couldn't stay where she was for a moment longer.

"Where are you going, Bodel?" Miss Dobson had finished her conversation with the other teacher and turned her attention back to the team.

Bodel had already been in trouble once that day for ignoring a member of staff. She had just enough sense left not to make the same mistake a second time. "I'm not feeling too good, Miss. May I be excused?" Bodel responded.

Miss Dobson could sense that something was not right, so she excused Bodel with strict instructions to go to the student information center so that they could keep an eye on her. Bodel left PE early that day and went to sit down in the student information center. She was not sick at all, but she lay down on the stretcher bed with an ice pack on her forehead, desiring for the day to end.

"How are you feeling, young lady?" Miss Jules asked. That was the lady who worked in the student information center. She was a kind-hearted, soft-spoken lady who had a slight naivety about her. Whenever kids came to the student information center, she mothered them.

"I'm doing slightly better," Bodel replied, looking at the clock as she pressed the melting ice pack against the side of her forehead. Bodel reasoned that if she could just stay in the center for an extra ten minutes, then they wouldn't bother sending her back outside to PE.

"Would you like me to give your mum a call?" Miss Jules asked with compassion and sincerity.

That was a question that could have caused an already unstable girl to topple over the edge. The whispers in Bodel's head told her relentlessly that she didn't even have a mum. She suppressed those voices momentarily and replied with deceptive gratitude. "No, thanks, Miss Jules," Bodel began. "I'll be all right. Mum's coming to pick me up at the end of the day anyway."

"Okay, my dear, so long as you're sure," Miss Jules replied.

Bodel smiled and nodded as she rested her half-closed eyes.

The last thing that Bodel wanted was Aunt Maddie receiving a phone call from the school. She would know at once that Bodel was not ill. She would suspect something was wrong. Getting out of PE was enough of a treat for Bodel that day. She was not feeling her usual self, and the last thing she wanted was to be outside with a pair of shorts and a T-shirt in the bitter cold. Bodel put her head down for an additional ten minutes, grasping securely the almost-melted ice pack that she had initially requested to cool her head down.

"I'm feeling much better now," Bodel announced as she jumped off the bed she was resting on. She had calculated just enough time to go and change back into her school uniform so that Aunt Maddie would not suspect anything unusual had happened when she came to pick her up at the end of the day. Miss Jules signed Bodel out of the student information center so she could go back to the changing room and get dressed for afternoon registration.

Chapter 8
Home Time

"Tick-tock, tick-tock. Such is the way of a grandfather clock," Bodel sang along in a quiet undertone as she sat gazing optimistically at the round plastic clock that hung on her classroom wall. It wasn't a grandfather clock at all; in fact, it was just an ordinary white plastic clock with a perfectly rounded plastic cover in the center and three hands underneath that pointed to the numbers.

It was afternoon registration. The school day was practically over.

"Clocks are a funny thing," Bodel thought aloud as she sat listening intently to the quiet ticking sound that filled the four corners of the room. "One hand points to the minute, the other points to the hour, and there's a third one that just keeps on moving forward every second," Bodel continued, sharing her thoughts with the quiet student next to her, Rhona.

Rhona didn't speak much; she was more of a listener. She usually sat next to Bodel in the center of the room during tutor time. Rhona was a bit of an introvert, but she had a very warm persona that attracted people like a magnet. Whenever Bodel had her random afternoon outpourings, Rhona usually just nodded along and smiled. She was an intelligent young girl with wisdom beyond her years; however, she came across as very shy. Rhona had neck-length, straight brown hair, brown skin, and round piercing eyes. Whenever she looked at someone, it was as if she was actually looking straight through them. She always sat with what could be perceived as an expression of anxiety on her face, but when she spoke, she had the most pleasant, calming voice. Rhona was a very mysterious girl, but she made Bodel feel at ease.

Bodel used to find Rhona very strange, the way she sat in silence and hardly ever spoke. That's how certain people would describe Bodel as well. Rhona was different, though; she was almost mute with her silence. Because Rhona was so quiet, no one really knew what was going on with her. If there was one thing that this experience of finding out that she was adopted had taught Bodel, it was that you can never judge anyone by what they display on the outside. There was always more to a person than met the eye. Bodel continued studying the hands on the clock as she spoke.

"Time is a funny thing; it's forever going forwards, but never backwards." This was something that Bodel had quickly come to realize. No matter how much she sat and pondered the past, she had to forget the things that were behind her and continue to move forward, just like the hands of the clock that caught her eye. Bodel had to reach forward for better days—whatever they were. Bodel knew that she couldn't change the past. Her adoptive mother always used to say that there was no use crying over spilled milk. She would always tell Bodel to live in the present and not worry about tomorrow because tomorrow would take care of itself. These days, Bodel wondered whether these snippets of wisdom were just preparation for the news that was to come.

Afternoon form time was one of the longest ten minutes of a short school day. It was the time when everyone just sat staring at the clock, waiting to be released.

"Bodel, you have a message at the school reception," announced an unexpected voice that had just come into the classroom.

"What could this be about?" Bodel pondered. "Who could be leaving a message for me?" Bodel asked her questions in a slow, cautious voice as she gradually made her way out of the classroom.

Crippling thoughts began to seep into her mind. Bodel began to panic; she went into a state of extreme anxiety as negative thoughts pierced their way towards the inner part of her mind. Bodel prepared herself to expect the worst. Anytime she heard that news was coming, she always assumed that there was going to be some kind of letdown, or bad news, or illness. She told herself that if she always expected the worst, then she could never be disappointed again.

Bodel paced down the corridor and arrived at the front of the school reception to be told that her mother had called. Well, they must have meant her adoptive mother, Aunt Maddie, because as far as Bodel knew, her real mother had passed away shortly after she was born. Aunt Maddie had called in to pass on a message that she would not be able to pick Bodel up from school because she had been called into Elisa's primary school; Elisa had been unwell that day. Elisa was Bodel's youngest sister, the last of five children.

"I guess Aunt Maddie can't put all of her attention on me; she has four other children to think about," Bodel supposed with a fatigued voice. The cheerful receptionist gave her a pitiful half smile as she handed her the folded yellow Post-it note with the message scribbled down in faded blue ink.

"There you go, dear," the receptionist said, speaking softly but with a high-pitched undertone.

The note read: I won't be able to pick you up this afternoon, sweetheart. Please go straight home after school. Lots of love, Mum.

Bodel read the note with an air of contempt. She didn't know whether it was the adorning use of the word sweetheart that added to her ever-increasing infuriation or just the rippling effect of the deep sense of rejection that she wanted so desperately to be free from.

Bodel knew that it was unreasonable for her to feel this way. Surely, if Elisa was ill, then Aunt Maddie would have to go and tend to her. It didn't mean that Bodel was unloved; it didn't justify the overpowering feeling of rejection that was rising up inside her body as she stood tightly gripping the folded Post-it note that had just been handed to her. It slipped Bodel's mind that she was standing in front of the school receptionist because, in reality, she was wrestling with conflicting thoughts of negativity. She was having a full-blown conversation within her mind.

"Thank you," Bodel exhaled as she sauntered away from the glass window at the reception desk. Bodel strolled back down the corridor to her form room to collect her schoolbag.

The final bell had rung by then, and everyone had left the classroom in order to make their way home. Bodel rambled her way back through the crowds of excited students who were eager to burst back through the school gates and start their weekend. Once again a chattering sound filled the air as girls discussed what they were going to wear to the party on Saturday and what color glitter they were going to use to decorate their faces. The boys chased each other down the corridors, almost running as they walked. Bodel was not interested in the party or the glitter. She just wanted to go home and retreat underneath her covers.

As she got to the door of her classroom, Nina was there waiting for her. "What was all that about?" Nina inquired with a nosey yet somehow compassionate voice.

"Nothing," Bodel replied with an increasing sense of unease as she clamped down on her feelings once again. "Mum can't pick me up today, so she just called in to let me know that I need to go straight home." Bodel rolled her eyes as she spoke to create the impression that it was no big deal.

"I told her that I can make my own way home," she continued, as if to imply that she was tired of her mother's overbearing shows of affection.

Inside, Nina just wanted to shake her head and walk away; she was tired of Bodel's pretense, but something inside her tugged at her heart and told her to be patient. That was her conscience. "Okay," Nina continued with an increasingly excited tone. "Shall we walk together then?"

Bodel thought about it for a short minute. She had been avoiding Nina all day, and if she walked home with her now, Nina would probably want to know what she had been doing for the past week and why she hadn't picked up her phone.

The panic started again. "It's all going to come out," Bodel reasoned within her teenage mind. "If I walk home with Nina, she is going to find out everything."

Bodel didn't really understand why she felt the need to keep her feelings bottled up. Nina was her best friend. Surely she would be able to understand. Deep down, Bodel knew that what she was doing was strange, but she was more frightened than anything else. If she admitted to Nina that her mother was not her mother, then she would have to come to terms with the fact that her real mother had died. No one had mentioned her father, so she didn't know where to begin with him.

Bodel felt that if she kept everything to herself, then she could somehow pretend that it had never happened. More than anything else, Bodel feared having to come face-to-face with the truth. She had been living under a fog for so long that she thought she had learned to see clearly, even under there. That's the thing with fog—it clouds a person's vision and presents an atmosphere in which self-deception can be widely cultivated. Oftentimes, when people cannot see clearly, they start distorting situations and retelling stories to themselves in ways that never happened. Once Bodel got used to deceiving herself, she found it easier to deceive others. She told herself that her mother was out there somewhere, but she just hadn't met her yet.

Bodel realized that once she started telling Nina the truth about her life, then she would have to deal with that same truth herself. She was not ready to face the truth just yet. Bodel was not ready to grieve the death of her mother even though she knew she needed to. She felt it was safer to keep her feelings locked up.

Bodel's suppressed grief, however, was already starting to manifest itself in strange ways. Whenever she toyed with the idea of confiding in Nina, an uncontrollable sense of discomfort began to bubble inside her heart, so she suppressed it. She found it strange; she found the idea of grieving for her mother absolutely absurd. After all, how does a person grieve for someone that they didn't even know? Although Bodel wrestled with thoughts of guilt and rejection, she felt that she could not overcome them.

Bodel decided to quietly decline Nina's offer to accompany her on her homeward journey. "Being fifteen is complicated," Bodel concluded as she started her introverted journey to the place she once called home.

Chapter 9
I AM the Father

On her way home, Bodel decided to stop at the school library. It was in an ancient-looking building not far from the main building of the school. Bodel decided to stop there, not necessarily because she loved reading, but mainly because she wanted a place of peace and quiet to think about how she was going to navigate the remainder of her school life, and how she was going to find herself once again.

Although no one had mentioned Bodel's father to her, there was a large and active part of her brain that was buzzing with ever-growing curiosity regarding him. She wanted to know who he was. Bodel reasoned within her mind that if she found out who her father was, then she would be in a better position to find out who she was. She didn't even know where or how to begin. How does a person begin to search for a father? Is a library really the best place to start? Bodel stood in the midst of the tall, towering bookshelves, feeling both naive and clueless.

The simplest thing to do would be to ask Aunt Maddie, but Bodel didn't know how to start such a sensitive conversation. She didn't understand why Aunt Maddie had never mentioned her father when she spoke of her mother's tragic death.

Now that Bodel knew the truth, she was unsure of what it felt like to have a "real," biological father. She had grown up with parents who were actually her adoptive parents, Uncle Luis and Aunt Maddie. They had four biological children—Ted, Jacob,

Rayleigh, and Elisa. Ted was the oldest of all the children. He had moved out when Bodel was twelve years old, when he started university. Other than his sporadic visits home for food and money, she and the rest of the family didn't see Ted much. Jacob was just over a year older than Bodel. They used to attend the same secondary school, but they had very different friends. Jacob was quiet and extremely academic. Bodel found him to be quite the computer geek at times. Oftentimes, they had walked home from school together, but Jacob had become very independent ever since he started college. Most days it was just Bodel, Rayleigh, and Elisa at home.

Uncle Luis wasn't around the house that much. Most evenings, he worked late as a customs control officer in Heathrow Airport. He would usually come home weary and exhausted and then fall asleep on the couch. Bodel could tell that Aunt Maddie wasn't happy with all the late nights, but she didn't say much about it. She just kind of smiled and kept her head down. Bodel once overheard a phone conversation between Uncle Luis and Aunt Maddie that seemed to be quite heated.

"You're never home; I never get any help from you," Aunt Maddie began with a whimpering voice. Then there was a long pause in which Aunt Maddie yawned and sighed noisily. Bodel could not hear what Uncle Luis was saying on the other end of the phone, but shortly after the long pause, Aunt Maddie said, "Do whatever you want." She then put the phone down and started vacuuming.

It wasn't any wonder that Bodel was not in much of a hurry to go home. Early evenings at the Pascoe household were filled with one of two extremes, silence or quarrels.

After rummaging through the dusty wooden library shelves, Bodel had built up a satisfactory collection. She picked up her hefty pile of books and made her way to a quiet corner of the library, where she sat on a small brown leather beanbag. It was large enough to fit one person, and there was just enough room on the carpeted floor to rest her book tower.

Bodel liked to sit unaccompanied in the library. She perched comfortably under the warm orange lighting of the floor lamps. Surrounded by the soothing smell of chestnut wood, she immersed herself in a world of books. Happily she sat churning through the paper leaves, greatly indulging herself in an array of heartwarming tales about fatherhood. She started off by reading books about fathers—fiction books, nonfiction books, and even Bible stories.

Aunt Maddie wasn't that religious, but she used to read Bible stories to the children before they went to sleep. Bodel remembered the stories well, and her favorite one was about Noah and the ark. It was about a time when God decided He was going to flood the earth because people were doing such evil things in His sight and in His name. God decided to save Noah and his family, so He told Noah to build an ark that would float on the waters when the earth was flooded. The earth was flooded for 150 days, but Noah and his family remained safe inside the ark.

Bodel loved that story. She was always fascinated by God's love for Noah and Noah's obedience to God. She was amazed at the fact that he was able to build an ark that could save so many people and animals from an outpouring of rain that flooded the earth. Bodel could have done with an ark right about now, she thought—just somewhere that she could go to escape from her current life and start all over again.

As Bodel continued to make her way through the pile of books, a warm, tickly feeling embraced her heart. She remembered how Aunt Maddie always used to tell her bedtime stories and talk about a God in the Bible. She always used to say, "He is a good Father, and He puts the solitary in families."

Bodel had never really understood why Aunt Maddie kept on making that comment. Every time she spoke about the God in the Bible, Aunt Maddie would say, "He puts the solitary in families." Perhaps that was Aunt Maddie's way of edging towards the day when she would finally tell Bodel that she was part of the "solitary," and God had placed her in a family.

All at once, the old bedtime stories came toppling to the front of Bodel's mind. "He puts the solitary in families." Those words began to echo in her ears. However, Bodel wondered why God hadn't just kept her in her own family to begin with.

Just as that troubling thought climbed its way into Bodel's mind, a young girl came and stood in the midst of Bodel's carefully fenced-off area of the library. "Mind if I join you?" asked the girl in a soft, startling voice.

Bodel lifted her eyes from the page of her book and saw Rhona. Bodel looked at her, not knowing what to say. She was both shocked and unnerved. Rhona's soft voice startled Bodel because she had not expected anyone to come into her quiet, secluded area of the library. Bodel had purposely tucked herself away, hoping not to be disturbed.

"Are you reading the Bible?" Rhona continued. That was one of the few times Rhona had started a conversation with Bodel without any prior prompting.

"Yes, I am. I love the stories in here," Bodel replied, still rather panicky and unsure why Rhona had become so interested in her.

"Me too; I love the stories," Rhona continued in a voice full of enthusiasm. "I started reading the Bible to help with my religion and philosophy coursework, but now I'm just making my way through the stories."

"What are you reading at the moment?" Bodel inquired, now intrigued by the conversation. It seemed that they had found a common ground on which to connect; this was a change from Rhona's nodding away at Bodel's abstract analogies.

"Joseph and his technicolor dream coat," Rhona answered, as she began to edge herself away from the conversation. The countenance on Bodel's face, however, caused Rhona to pause.

For the first time in ages, Bodel felt comfortable speaking to someone about her life. Rhona sat down on the floor next to Bodel, who was now pleasantly surprised by her company. "Can I ask you something personal?" Bodel queried, not knowing where her sudden display of openness had come from.

"Yes, you can. What is it?" Rhona asked with open ears.

"Is there something the matter with me if I don't want to grieve?" Bodel continued.

"Grieve over what?" Rhona asked curiously.

"What if I don't want to grieve over the loss of my mother?" Bodel blurted this out with a sudden explosion that caused Rhona to gasp louder than she had ever spoken.

"Your mother died?" she continued, with sympathetic attentiveness.

Immediately Bodel became aware of what she was saying, but she didn't care; she just continued. As she began to speak, her voice cracked, the crack turned to a whimper, and the whimper turned into a loud sob. There she sat, in the corner of the library, pouring out her heart like water rushing through a floodgate.

She told Rhona the story of how her birth mother had passed away just after she was born, and how no one had spoken about her father.

"I don't even know where I belong anymore," Bodel sobbed, with her head buried in her hands. "I have no family; I have no friends."

Rhona paused and looked at her, not knowing what to say. Then she said something that Bodel never expected. A piece of the puzzle fell into place that helped Bodel understand her own sudden desire to open up to Rhona after she had been so reluctant to tell anyone about this.

"I live with my mother; it's just the two of us now. Last year, we went on a family holiday to Italy. My dad went with us, but he got really ill while we were there." As Rhona began to tell her story, her eyes began to well up with tears, but she held herself together well, unlike Bodel, who was now sobbing uncontrollably.

"That was the last time I ever saw him." Rhona spoke in a droning voice, her piercing eyes looking straight ahead.

"I'm so sorry to hear that," Bodel said in a quivering voice. She sat in astonishment at the divulgence of detail that Rhona had just bestowed upon her. For a moment, there was nothing but silence, broken only by the rustling of paper as Rhona reached inside her bag.

"What are you looking for?" Bodel inquired.

Rhona reverted back to her pleasant, soundless exterior as she smiled. She didn't answer Bodel straight away, but she began scribbling words down on a piece of paper. It looked a bit like a poem. When she finished, she handed it to Bodel. Whether Rhona realized it or not, the words in the poem jumped out at

Bodel and filled her fragmented heart with a satisfaction that she had never felt before.

"This is something that my mother gave to me after my father passed away. I wrote these words down, and I read them every morning."

Rhona had handed Bodel a neatly folded sheet of beige, patterned paper with a short inscription in the middle. As Bodel began to read the poetic words, they immediately began to resonate within her heart. Bodel read the words out loud:

My child, I made you,
In My own image I made you.
And you are fearfully and wonderfully made.
I AM the Father and I make no mistake,
For I AM the Potter and you are My clay,
And I have molded you.
I AM He who chips away at your transgressions;
As far as the east is from the west,
I have removed your transgressions from you,
And I have blotted out your sins
And your lawless deeds for My own sake.
For you are Mine, and you belong to Me,
and I have accepted you.

These powerful words spoke to Bodel like an audible voice, filling the emptiness inside her heart with hope once again. To know that she was loved and accepted by an all-powerful Father was enough for her.

"You can keep that," said Rhona with a smile. "Read it every morning, just like I do."

Bodel didn't say anything; she didn't need to. Rhona understood. Kind words, so swiftly spoken, had the power to change Bodel's life forever.

"I have to go now, but I'll see you soon." And with that, Rhona disappeared.

Bodel remained in the same spot for a while, staring steadily at the words in the note that Rhona had given to her. She repeated the endearing words to herself once more before she folded the paper into fourths and placed it neatly in the side compartment of her school rucksack.

"We are closing in five minutes," announced a soft and patient voice. It was the librarian.

With that, Bodel scrambled through her stack of books and chose a few that she could continue to read at home. "I am fearfully and wonderfully made," she told herself once more as she chose a classic novel to go along with her daily dose of Bible-story reading.

There was an inscription on the inside cover of Bodel's borrowed Bible. Written neatly with a thick black ink pen, it read, "You are fearfully and wonderfully made."

Although Bodel didn't know who wrote the message or why it was still there on the inside cover of her library book, she felt a deep conviction in her heart that the message was written for her.

Bodel reverted back to her timid self for a moment. She felt that this was something she couldn't tell anyone. They would think she was crazy. Words on the cover of a library book that were written just for her—it was almost surreal. But there was something about the inscription that matched the words of Rhona's poem. There was something special about that inscription in the library book, something about those words that caused them to spring forth and reverberate in Bodel's heart and mind. She felt comfortable in her own skin again.

Bodel gave a smile of contentment that remained on her face as she closed her borrowed Bible and made her way towards the counter. Neatly she packed it inside her bag alongside her slightly worn copy of Jane Eyre. With a rucksack full of books and a mind full of positive thoughts, Bodel left the library and started to make her way home.

Chapter 10
I Am Bodel

As Bodel stepped outside the shelter of the library and peered into the misty streets, she began to contemplate all that had just taken place. She felt different now—her mind was lighter. No longer was she being tormented by thoughts of abandonment and uncertainty. She realized that her identity was not defined by what people thought about her or who she pretended to be in order to keep up appearances. She realized that she was loved by an omnipresent God who had created her perfectly and loved her dearly. Being adopted didn't mean that she was rejected; it meant that she was loved, and it wasn't something that she needed to be ashamed of.

Bodel had grieved that day in the library. She had finally grieved and felt guiltless while doing so. She realized that grieving was not a sign of weakness; it was a sign of strength. It allowed her to accept what had happened and to find healing.

"I am Bodel," she told herself as she clambered down the library steps and across the concrete pathway that led towards the main road. "I am loved and accepted," she continued as she travelled in the direction of her house, lugging her heavy rucksack on one shoulder.

It was five thirty, and the sun had fallen a little lower in the sky. It was early winter, but it felt as though a warm summer breeze blew through Bodel's hair. The streets were busy and congested as usual. Bodel strolled along, contemplating whether to go home or find another quiet, secluded place to continue reading.

Bodel did not realize just how powerful words could be until her constant repetition of "I am fearfully and wonderfully made" chased every menacing thought from her previously suffering mind. "I'm not just a reject," she told herself with a grin of satisfaction that cracked her cheeks and soothed her heart. The sweet feeling of serenity consumed her for the first time since she heard the news of her adoption, news that had seemed to rob her of every sense of self.

"I'm not a reject or a mistake!" she yelled gleefully as she continued her homeward stroll, with a newfound skip in her step.

From the corner of her eye, Bodel caught a glimpse of a homeless man. He was standing on the street corner and wearing a worn trench coat that reached the ground. He had pale, phantom-white skin; gray stringy hair that reached the nape of his neck; and the strangest silver-speckled beard that Bodel had ever seen in her fifteen years of life. She tried to hurry past him, hoping that he wouldn't notice her or try to make conversation with her. He looked frightening.

Bodel had to catch herself. She thought she might be hallucinating—it was broad daylight, and she found herself scurrying along a congested street trying to avoid a phantom silver-bearded man. "Pull yourself together, Bodel," she told herself as she continued strolling at a reasonably unconcerned pace, making her way home.

If there was one thing Bodel remembered, it was that you cannot judge anyone purely by outward appearance alone. She knew this more than anything because she had spent the majority of her day trying to be something she was not. She had spent the better part of her week in denial. She knew the truth and her adoptive family knew the truth, but somehow she had felt bound to keep up the pretense in front of her friends.

At that moment, Bodel came face-to-face with herself. She was faced with the grave reality that she had been self-absorbed, selfish, inconsiderate. She stood as still as a statue in the middle of the pavement, clutching her rucksack close to her chest, as it had begun to weigh down her shoulder. With her right hand, she searched the right side of her jacket pocket, rummaging around for some tissue with which to wipe away all evidence of her ego- tistical despair.

She wanted to cry—not just cry, but sob uncontrollably once again. However, this time it was not because she found out that she had grown up in a family of strangers, but because she re- alized that she had made herself a stranger in that family. She had purposely made her family home into a place of solitude and hostility, when it didn't need to be that way. She had not been placed there accidentally. God had placed her there because, "He puts the solitary in families."

Bodel realized just how ungrateful she had been; she had not thought her actions through at all. How could she be so quick to disown the woman who had taken her in from birth? This was the woman who had cradled her, bathed her, fed her, and loved her relentlessly as her very own. All at once, the suppressed tears sprang to the surface of Bodel's eyes, like an unleashed torrent of rain. She stood unashamedly lamenting on the corner of the street as she began to come to terms with just how unreasonable, selfish, and ungrateful she had been. She had started referring to her mother as an aunt, and she had been so full of pride and needless humiliation that she had lied to her best friend.

Bodel had known Nina since they were eight years old. They had gone to primary school together. She knew that Nina wouldn't shun her or treat her any differently just because she was adopted. Bodel had always known deep down that there really was no need to continue deceiving Nina; it was her multitude of insecurities that had convinced her to behave in such a way. As these thoughts filled Bodel's mind, she felt as though a heavy burden had been lifted from her shoulders. She was free at last.

With that passing thought, Bodel stopped and looked behind her to see whether the silver-bearded man was still there. He had moved into a seated position by that point. He was sitting, slightly shivering, on the bench next to where he initially had stood. Driven by compassion, Bodel went back and gave him the two golden pound coins that she had in her blazer pocket.

"Get yourself a sandwich," she said as she dropped the coins into the bowl on the ground next to the man.

"I would give you more, but that's all I have."

The silver-bearded man smiled and looked at Bodel.

"Every little bit helps," he replied, astonished by her kindness.

Then she continued through the busy, congested streets and went straight through the extended piece of greenery that led to her house.

Chapter 11
Is My Father Still Alive?

As Bodel approached the front gate of her house, she began to reminisce about the events of the day. She had left her house carrying a heavy weight of turmoil and returned light as a feather. Bodel marched blissfully up to the front door, peeping through the window to see whether anyone was home yet. Having seen that the lights were out and it was pitch- black inside, Bodel reached for the spare key in the secret compartment of the mailbox. It was always kept inside a tightly sealed money box with a numerical code that only the family knew. She let herself inside.

Back at home, Bodel sat curled up on her living room sofa. It was warm and soft and neatly decorated with blue velvet cushions. The walls were full of pictures—portraits and souvenirs from all their family holidays. There was one particular photograph that caught Bodel's attention. It was from their family vacation to the south of France last summer, one of the best family holidays that Bodel had been on. She remembered the pleasantly warm weather and the striking, golden-brown sand that tickled her feet. It had felt like a piece of paradise.

The buildings were tall and close together, not so close that they were cramped, but rather perfectly ordered like a row of toy blocks that had been put together by an ingenious child. They weren't brown, bricked, and ordinary, but carefully decorated with an array of vibrant colors—flushed pink and creamy beige— and the sky was a calm blue splattered with a pure-white mist. In front of the buildings was a small family of palm trees overlooking the golden, sandy beach neatly situated by a turquoise-green sea. Bodel could see clearly now—her memories were as clear as the tropical ocean that now flooded and infiltrated her mind. She had grown up amongst beautiful buildings, all different shapes and sizes, but each one glistening in its own unique way.

Keys rattling outside the living room window broke Bodel's trip down memory lane. Bodel could hear Rayleigh and Elisa's excited voices as they raced up the pathway to the front door. Elisa sounded like her usual vibrant self. Bodel remained perched on the sofa until they peered their little heads around the corner of the corridor and screamed, "Hey, sis!" while running up the stairs.

"How was your day?" Bodel's mother asked inquisitively. "Sorry I couldn't come and pick you up." Bodel had not forgotten about the incident with the vice principal earlier, but she certainly wasn't going to bring it up if the news had not reached her parents just yet.

"That's okay, Mum," she smiled. "I made my way home, and I had an all right day." Bodel didn't want to exaggerate; her day was all right other than the detention she received from the vice principal for refusing to follow instructions from a member of staff.

Putting that to one side, Bodel contemplated whether to tell her mother--Aunt Maddie--about the note that Rhona had given her in the library or whether she should just keep it to herself.

"I made a new friend at the library," Bodel began. "I made a new friend who showed me that I am fearfully and wonderfully made." She was so excited to share the news with her mother—Aunt Maddie—that she forgot about the repercussions of her detention for a moment.

"Okay . . .," Aunt Maddie replied with a look of confusion. "What's your friend's name?" she continued.

"He's called I AM," Bodel replied as she brought the neatly folded paper from the side wallet of her bag.

Aunt Maddie read the note with a sober expression on her face. It looked like a child's writing.

"Who wrote this?" Aunt Maddie inquired.

"Rhona gave it to me," Bodel explained. "She said that I should read it every morning."

Aunt Maddie skimmed over the words approvingly and handed it back to Bodel with a look of contentment that spread across her face. "That's wonderful, sweetheart," she said in a soft tone as she lugged her shopping bags to the kitchen. "I'm glad," Aunt Maddie concluded with a smile.

Aunt Maddie made her way to the kitchen to get dinner ready, and Bodel remained curled up on the sofa, plowing her way through her mini-pile of books that she had brought home from the library. Jacob wasn't home from college yet. Rayleigh and Elisa were upstairs preoccupied with their PlayStation games, and Uncle Luis was at work as usual. The house was peaceful and the atmosphere was serene.

"It's dinnertime!" Aunt Maddie yelled with a gleeful voice that filled every corner of their two-story house. At dinnertime, everyone would usually collect their food and eat it in different areas of the house while they were engrossed in their other activities. On this particular evening, however, they decided to sit around the table and eat dinner together.

Elisa wasn't at dinner that night; she was fast asleep, tucked away under the comfort of her duvet. Jacob wasn't home either, as he had called to say he was going out to the cinema with his friends straight after college. Much to Bodel's delight, Uncle Luis came home early that evening. He said it had been a quiet day at the airport and some of the staff were let off early. He joined them for dinner.

Bodel sat twirling her spaghetti and meatballs around her plate, taking slow, lingering slurps, and eating her vegetables with delight. Her appetite had slowly returned, and she found herself sitting on the chair without feeling the need to check whether the legs were stable. Sitting at the dinner table was both an endearing and enduring ritual. Bodel contemplated whether or not this was an appropriate time to inquire as to the where-abouts of her father.

It was a strange topic that everyone avoided. Bodel glanced at Rayleigh, who sat opposite an empty plate, gulping down her small glass of orange juice. Patiently Bodel sat hoping that once Rayleigh left the kitchen, the atmosphere would become more conducive to serious conversation. She was hoping for an at-mosphere where truths could be told, information could be re-vealed, and answers could be provided. Rayleigh was only eight years old; there was no need for her to be a partaker in such adult-like exchanges, Bodel reasoned as a responsible big sister.

"Mum, I'm finished," Rayleigh announced as she jumped off her seat in a hurry.

"Make sure you change into your pajamas once you get up-stairs, sweetheart," Aunt Maddie reminded Rayleigh as she creaked open the dining room door.

"Yes, Mum," Rayleigh replied as she skipped up the stairs.

Then there were three. Uncle Luis was quiet at the table. It was a strange quietness, as though he had something to say but was trying to choose his words carefully.

"How was school today, Bodel?" he began with the fatherly affection that reminded Bodel of the early days of her childhood. Bodel was suddenly reminded of the days when her father—Uncle Luis—would take the time to sit down and listen to her and ask about her day with genuine interest. Those days had become a faint memory now. She suspected that something was up; there was unease in his voice.

"Your school called," Uncle Luis continued. Bodel knew there had to be a catch; she could not remember the last time that Uncle Luis had showed genuine interest in her life. Searching her memory, she could not recall the last time he had actually asked her about her day at school or whether she even went to school. Uncle Luis just didn't want the disturbance or the embarrassment of receiving phone calls from the school.

"What did they say?" Bodel asked with a stuttering terror in her voice. She knew why they had called but wanted to avoid the scolding that was to come.

"You tell me!" Uncle Luis replied in a hostile tone.

Bodel went on to explain the incident that had happened with her English teacher. She didn't say anything about PE because, as far Bodel was aware, the violent attack on Tia Peterson had happened only in her mind.

Aunt Maddie had stopped speaking at this point. She looked at Bodel with a stare of disappointment. Uncle Luis didn't say much, but his silence was more painful than a thousand words.

"What has gotten into you, Bodel?" Aunt Maddie's line of questioning was so unnerving that it caused Bodel's heart to shake from the inside of her chest. Bodel stopped speaking for a moment, but then she screamed at the top of her voice—a loud, shrill scream that caused the ceiling to tremble. Well, at least that's how it sounded to Bodel. All she really did was let out a flat and defeated exhale. She felt like no one understood her. She started to shrink inside her own thoughts once again. They had told her that her mother had died, they never mentioned her father, and now they were asking her what had gotten into her. Bodel felt that it was absolutely ridiculous. She wanted them to know exactly what had gotten into her.

A sudden, inquisitive boldness came over Bodel as she shook off every terrifying thought that had found its place within her mind. She wanted to know where her birth father was. She wanted to ask a million questions; curiosity was eating her up inside. She had a right to know what had happened to her father, didn't she? This was her chance.

"Can I ask you a question?" Bodel blurted out, looking Aunt Maddie straight in the eye.

"Of course," said Aunt Maddie hesitatingly. It was almost as if she could read Bodel's mind and she knew what was coming. "You can ask me anything. Whether I'll be able to answer it or not is a different story, my dear," she added.

"Well . . . when you sat me down the other day to tell me what happened to my mother," Bodel began in an inquiring tone, "it's just that . . . well, you never mentioned my father. I just want to know, is my father still alive?"

Bodel asked the question, and then her voice fell silent. Her eyes gazed expectantly at Aunt Maddie, anticipating her response. Uncle Luis barely looked up. He pretended to be preoccupied with clearing his plate from the dining room table. Clearly, there was some sort of taboo that surrounded this line of questioning, Bodel thought. Nonetheless, she persisted on bringing it to the surface. She had a right to know where her father was, or so she thought.

The disheartened look on Aunt Maddie's face spoke more than a thousand words. Bodel glanced over at Uncle Luis, who remained emotionless. They had already told her that her mother was dead. Surely there was nothing worse than that, Bodel thought.

Before the crippling thoughts could intrude further in her mind, Bodel reminded herself of the words that I AM had spoken to her earlier that day in the library: "You are Mine, and you belong to Me, and I have accepted you." With that, she knew that she was loved, cared for, and accepted, so it didn't matter what news Aunt Maddie and Uncle Luis had concerning her father. She just wanted to know where he was. She just wanted answers.

"Is my father still alive?" she repeated, with a more obstinate undertone.

Bodel was conscious that this adamant tone might unnerve Uncle Luis, but the unspoken truth was that their father-daughter relationship had pretty much disintegrated over the past seven years anyway. Bodel had no idea how Uncle Luis felt about her wanting to meet her birth father or whether he was completely indifferent to the whole idea. Nevertheless, this was something that Bodel wanted to do for herself.

"Yes, Bodel, your father is alive," Uncle Luis answered this time.

"Then I want to see him," she said. With that, the room fell silent. Uncle Luis and Aunt Maddie looked at each other for a short minute; they paused and looked at Bodel together.

"Does he not want to see me?" Bodel persisted in her line of inquiry. "Does he even know about me?" she continued. Aunt Maddie and Uncle Luis could see that Bodel was going to be persistent, very persistent, and that she was not about to give up anytime soon.

"You said that my mother was a close friend of yours," she said, looking at Aunt Maddie as she asked this question. "Were you friends with my father too?" she continued.

"No, dear," Aunt Maddie replied. "We knew of him, but I wouldn't say that we were close friends," she continued.

"So what happened to him?" Bodel continued. "Why hasn't anyone told me what happened to my father?" She was now a confident participant in this conversation.

"Listen, sweetheart . . . the adoption agency did give us the contact details for your father, but the thing is, at the time that we adopted you, he was . . . he was in prison," Aunt Maddie continued.

"Prison?" Bodel gasped in astonishment.

Once again an air of enigmatic silence consumed the atmosphere around the dining room table. Outside was a dense black; the sky was blank and starless. There was a blanket of darkness that covered the streets, except for one minuscule speck of light that came from a lonesome street lamp situated to the north of the Pascoe's semidetached home. The lonesome street lamp shed its ray of light on the small section of the pavement just outside the front gate of the Pascoe house—just in front of the shrub bush. The once-congested streets were still and lifeless; the howling wind had turned to a whisper.

"Yes, dear, he was in prison," Aunt Maddie replied, choosing every word carefully before she spoke.

Bodel wanted to keep asking questions, but she made herself stop. She reasoned within herself that sometimes too much information was more than was necessary. She refused to keep on digging for the how and the why and decided to focus on the where.

"I would like to meet my father." She made the statement in a monotone voice and left it there.

Bodel couldn't quite grasp what had come over her. She wasn't angry or bitter or resentful anymore. She didn't want to know what her father had done or why he was in prison. Surprisingly enough, she didn't even blame herself as she would have previously done. Even when it was quite obvious that the events of life were completely outside her control, there was a former part of Bodel that had always found a way to blame herself. She would then allow herself to fall into a deep sense of depression, but now she had found a new source of strength. Rejection could no longer take root in her so easily. She did not water the feeling of rejection or allow it to grow.

"Okay . . .," Aunt Maddie continued with a slightly resistant tone. It was as if she was answering and withholding information both at the same time. "Are you absolutely sure?" she continued.

"Yes," Bodel replied. "I would like to see my father."

Bodel uttered those words with an undeniable boldness and conviction that left no room for any misinterpretation. She knew exactly what she was asking.

"If my father is still alive, then I would like to see him," she said for the final time.

Aunt Maddie and Uncle Luis looked at each other and nodded in agreement. They could see that something had changed inside this daughter of theirs. They had kept certain things out of Bodel's sphere of knowledge in order to protect her, but she seemed so settled in this matter. Her confidence was such that it assured them that the time was right for Bodel to meet this father that she was so persistent in seeing.

"We will see what we can do," Uncle Luis replied after a long pause. "We will most certainly try our best for you."

The street lamp outside flickered in the nightfall, and the discussion came to an end. Aunt Maddie turned her attention to drying the washed cutlery that was placed neatly on a plate rack in the kitchen. Uncle Luis sat motionless and quiet.

"I'm going to bed now," Bodel said in a voice that broke the lingering silence. "I don't want to be late to school tomorrow," she added.

Her new sense of direction was both rejuvenating and perplexing to Aunt Maddie and Uncle Luis, but they rested in the knowledge that they had always known this day would come.

With that, Bodel skipped lightly up the stairs and retired to her room. Sitting in the center of her perfectly dressed bed, she once again unfolded the liberating note that I AM had given her, and she read it aloud to herself:

My child, I made you,
In My own image I made you.
And you are fearfully and wonderfully made,
I AM the Father and I make no mistake,
For I AM the Potter and you are My clay,
And I have molded you.

Is My Father Still Alive?

I AM He who chips away at your transgressions,
So far as the East is from the West,
I have removed your transgressions from you.
And I have blotted out your sins
And your lawless deeds for my own sake.
For you are Mine, and you belong to Me,
and I have accepted you.

"I am Bodel," she said aloud, with a confident self-assurance that made her feel at ease in her entirety. The soothing exchange of affection transitioned Bodel into a deep and peaceful sleep. She felt rejuvenated and ready for whatever was to come next.

Chapter 12
Confession Time

Early the following morning, Bodel woke up with a pounding headache that felt like a drum beating against the side of her head. She opened her eyes and closed them again before tossing and turning and forcing herself to her feet. Bodel threw her fleecy blanket onto her crumpled bedsheets and bolted down the stairs at the speed of light.

Rapidly she rummaged through the kitchen cupboard where the painkillers were kept. Bodel had decided that nothing was going to keep her from school that day. There was a sign on the painkiller packet that said "take only with food," so Bodel pulled a banana from the bunch in the fruit bowl, wolfed it down, and washed down two painkillers with a gulp of water. She ran back upstairs and buried her head in her pillow. Gripping tightly to the sides of her pillow, she prayed earnestly that her hammering headache would disappear.

It was seven o'clock in the morning, and her alarm had just gone off. Bodel hit the snooze button a couple of times, hoping a short power nap would be enough to dissipate her ever-increasing headache. Bodel soon fell back asleep.

Moments later she woke up to the sound of a bird cooing outside her window. She drew her frilled curtains to the side and gazed out. To her amazement, a pure-white dove had perched itself on the corner of the chestnut wood fence that surrounded the garden. The dove sat still, balancing on the corner of the fence and gazing earnestly into the distance. Its long, drawn-out coos sounded like laments. Bodel watched from her bedroom window, admiring its peaceful, gentle nature. It stayed in one position for a short while before it took off at the speed of light, its wings making a sharp whistling sound as it sailed through the skies. The dove fluttered into the vast maze of the airy sky and faded into the distance.

"What a beautiful sight to behold," Bodel exclaimed in a soft undertone, still in awe at the splendor of her morning. She twisted her neck from side to side and pressed the palm of her hand tightly against the front of her forehead. She let out a loud, soothing exhale as she grinned at the realization that her head was no longer pounding.

It was seven thirty. Bodel peeped out of her window into the bare greenery of the garden where the nettle had overgrown and the cracks in the fence were few and far between. That was an area where a warm ray of light neatly flickered on a patch of grass. The morning felt warm, although it was winter, and the clouds were toppling over each other. A gentle breeze caused the trees to whistle as the remnants of dawn came to a swift end and morning fully arrived.

Bodel decided that today was going to be a blissful day. Rayleigh and Elisa were up early. Bodel could hear them squabbling relentlessly in the room next door. She turned her music up to block out the noise and sat down to read the letter that Rhona had given her in the library.

"I am fearfully and wonderfully made." Looking into the mirror, she repeated the words out loud as she waited for the tap in the bathroom to stop running. The sound of running water was Bodel's way of knowing that the bathroom was occupied. Once the water stopped running, she knew that the bathroom was vacant and she could commence her morning routine.

While she was in the shower, Bodel continued to ponder the words from the "I AM" note, and she began to consider how she would share her stories with Nina later on at school. Fear and anxiety no longer saturated her mind; Bodel was comfortable with herself once again.

Dressed in her blue pleated skirt, cherry-red V-neck jumper, and a neatly aligned navy-blue blazer, Bodel was almost ready to start her day. She pulled on her knee-length socks and shiny black loafers to bring her outfit to completion. She made her way downstairs to see Rayleigh and Elisa eating their porridge around the breakfast table while Aunt Maddie paced frantically around the kitchen looking for something.

"Good morning, sweetheart," Aunt Maddie said as she took a break from her search to greet Bodel.

"Morning, Mum," Bodel replied as she took her seat at the breakfast table. It wasn't quite clear what Aunt Maddie was looking for. "What have you lost?" Bodel inquired while pouring milk into her cereal.

"I'm looking for my purse. I've been looking for it all morning," Aunt Maddie replied with a perplexed look on her face. Bodel could see a black suede purse resting on the corner of the microwave; it was almost impossible to miss.

"Isn't this your purse?" Bodel asked, pointing to the suede purse that was partly tucked behind a cloth on top of the microwave.

Startled, Aunt Maddie looked to where Bodel was pointing. "Yes, it is!" she exclaimed with a sigh of relief. "I have been looking everywhere for it."

Aunt Maddie had always told Bodel not to worry about things. Aunt Maddie said that sometimes the thing that you were looking for most anxiously was right there in front of you. If you just calmed down and stopped looking, then you would probably find it.

"Okay, let's go. It's time for school," Aunt Maddie started abruptly. She was a very time-conscious woman and never wanted to be late for anything. Aunt Maddie always told the children to organize themselves the night before, to have their clothes ready and their bags packed so that they would not be rushing around in the mornings. That was why she was so unnerved at the thought of misplacing her purse. One misplaced item would have ruined her entire schedule.

Aunt Maddie always seemed to enjoy the school run. She took a route that led her to Bodel's school first; then she went in a circular motion to drop off Rayleigh and Elisa before going back home. Aunt Maddie was an accountant by trade, but she had worked from home ever since Elisa was born. When the house was empty, she worked to get most of her work completed.

The drive to school seemed unusually short that morning, and Bodel was eager to get there. Aunt Maddie pulled up to the front of the school, and Bodel jumped out of the car, waving as she trotted away joyfully.

"I'll be back to pick you up at four thirty," Aunt Maddie reminded Bodel as she glanced back to acknowledge the reminder. On Mondays, Bodel finished school an hour later because she had netball enrichments.

"Okay, Mum," Bodel yelled, as she continued to walk with a bounce in her step.

Bodel stood on the playground, surrounded by an air of excitement. High-pitched screams pierced the atmosphere as students shared their stories and basked in the aftermath of the weekend's antics. It seemed that Bodel had missed out on an exciting party over the weekend, but that was of no importance to her. She had her own eventful weekend to think about.

Bodel scanned the playground, looking for Nina. She was keen to tell her about the Friend that she had met in the library and how He had changed her life. Nina was in the center of the playground, surrounded by a crowd of students who were laughing hysterically. She caught Bodel's eye and walked towards her.

"Hey, how was your weekend?" Nina asked inquisitively.

"It was eventful," Bodel replied as she walked towards a bench. Nina was strolling closely behind. "I've been meaning to tell you something," Bodel continued.

"Really?" Nina answered, as if she already knew what was coming.

Bodel told Nina about the Friend that she had met in the library and how much He had changed her life for the better.

"What's His name?" Nina asked with an interest that was both kind and sincere.

"I AM," Bodel replied with a look of satisfaction. "I just call Him I AM."

Baffled and bewildered, Nina sat listening with interest to all that Bodel had to say. She listened as Bodel told her about Aunt Maddie and how she had recently been told that Aunt Maddie was not her real mum. Bodel told Nina her whole life story as they sat in the secluded area of the playground where the oak tree had spread its branches far and wide.

Nina sat as still as a statue, listening to all that had transpired in Bodel's life these past few weeks. She gave no response except to nod and offer an amicable smile. "So, where is your mum?" Nina asked.

Bodel looked down as she muttered the last part of the story, "Well, my mother died just after I was born."

Nina's eyes began to tear up as she swallowed with a large gulp that sounded in her throat. "I'm so sorry to hear that, Bodz. I don't even know what to say," she continued as she reached for Bodel's hand as a sign of comfort.

"What about your dad?" she continued. "Where is he?"

"My father . . . well, apparently he was in prison when I was born. I don't know anything about him."

"Prison?" Nina gasped. She didn't know whether it was okay to continue crying as Bodel told the story with an emotionless expression on her face.

"Yes, prison," Bodel continued while looking down at the cold concrete floor beneath her feet.

The first bell rang; it was time to go in to form time. Nina stood up, wiping every tear from her shaken visage as they walked arm in arm into school. "I don't know how you do it," Nina said. "I would be a complete mess."

"I've had time to let it settle in," Bodel replied with a sigh of satisfaction. "Besides, I AM showed me how to get through this."

The classroom was different today during morning registration. It seemed empty, almost skeletal. Bodel made her way to her seat in the center of the room and sat patiently waiting for the morning announcements. Bodel was sitting at the table alone that morning; she assumed that Rhona was late that day. Bodel wanted to catch up with Rhona and talk about how much I AM had been helping her in the mornings and throughout her day. However, it didn't seem that Rhona was coming that day; Bodel reasoned that she must be ill. Then came the announcement: Rhona was gone. Miss Tulip, Bodel's form tutor, stood up and announced that Rhona had left the school and a new student would be joining the class later that afternoon.

Bodel didn't hear anything after the announcement that "Rhona left." Those were the words that stuck in her mind that morning; those were the words that echoed through her ears as she sat contemplating all the conversations they could've had. It's funny how people come in and out of your life so quickly.

Bodel sat still, scrolling through her mind, trying to recall whether Rhona had actually mentioned to her that she was going to be leaving school soon. The last time Bodel had seen Rhona was when they were in the library, and she certainly hadn't mentioned it that day. It was then Bodel realized just how precious time is. All that time Bodel was sitting next to Rhona at school, she never really got to know her. Maybe she could have, but Bodel never really listened—she spent most of the time talking. Life is a vapor—here today, gone tomorrow, literally.

The rest of the day was pretty much smooth sailing for Bodel, and Aunt Maddie came to pick her up at four thirty, as promised.

Chapter 13
Meeting My Father

Arriving home, Bodel noticed that Uncle Luis was home early once again. Rayleigh and Elisa were at an after-school club, and Jacob was out with his college friends as usual. The house was empty, and there was a foreign aroma that congested the atmosphere with a deep sense of agitation. Strangely, as Bodel entered the house, Aunt Maddie immediately motioned her towards the living room door.

"There's someone here that I would like you to meet," she said in a nervous tone that sounded quite peculiar.

A man sat on the living room sofa. He was tall when he stood, taller than Uncle Luis, and he had tightly curled hair much like Bodel's. His face was sharp and well-defined with a neatly chiseled beard, which ran across the sides of his face and bordered his chin. He looked like a man who had been carving out concrete and lifting heavy bricks on a construction site. Bodel moved towards him, taking small steps as she squinted. Her heart began to pound, and her sweat-filled palms clenched tightly together.

"Who are you?" Bodel inquired with a quivering voice. It was a question that she felt she already knew the answer to. Aunt Maddie didn't respond; she just gave a look of apprehension as she watched the scene play out before her eyes.

"Bonjour, comment allez-vous?" said the man. He spoke French fluently, with an accent that sounded almost native.

"Bonjour, je vais bien merci," Bodel replied with politeness and grace. "Who are you?" she asked, searching for clues in his expression.

"My name is Ethan Baptiste," he replied in a deep, husky voice. "So you must be Bodel," he added.

Bodel stood in awe, gazing at the strange man as if she were looking at her own reflection in the mirror. "Yes," she muttered as she smiled and looked up at him. "I am Bodel," she continued with cheerfulness and precision, still in awe of the tall stranger who stood in front of her.

"Are you my father?" she asked him with childlike apprehension. He nodded.

Then she turned to Aunt Maddie with glistening eyes. "So this is my father?" she asked.

"Yes, sweetheart, he is." And with that, Bodel was content.

She stood looking at her father, not knowing whether or not to embrace him, trying to make this moment last.

"Wow, so you're my father," she repeated under her breath as she stood in the center of the living room, still unable to completely comprehend the moment. Bodel was careful not to move in case she woke up and realized that this was all a dream. But it wasn't; this moment was as real as the night and day.

Her father's name was Ethan Baptiste. He was a Frenchman, born and raised just outside the French Alps. Ethan had moved to England when he met Bodel's mother. He had actually entered the UK illegally and was deported back to France not long before Bodel was born. That's where he served his time in prison.

As Bodel sat in the front room, she was both intrigued and absorbed in finding out more information about the man who sat in front of her. This was the first time she had ever seen a blood relative, and he was nothing like she had imagined. Bodel asked every question she could think of, but she was afraid to ask him why he had been in prison. She was afraid that she would find out something that she didn't want to know. She just wanted to forgive her father—forgive him for not contacting her all those years. She reasoned that it was probably better not to have too much detail.

Her curiosity, however, got the better of her. "Why didn't you try and contact me sooner?" she asked him.

"I knew that you were safe with Luis and Maddie. I had to respect their wishes; they said they would tell you about me once you turned fifteen. I was always here, Bodel. I was just waiting for you to ask about me," her father added.

Aunt Maddie and Uncle Luis stayed in the front room the whole time. It felt like a supervised visit, but that was fine with Bodel—she had nothing to hide. The nagging feeling of uncertainty had disappeared. Bodel had satisfied her own curiosity to an adequate level of contentment.

"I've got to get going now, Bodel, I've got to catch the last train back home." Ethan had traveled down on the Eurostar from his home in Marseille just to come and meet with Bodel. "But I'll see you again soon," he added.

She took one last glance at the man whom she had met in the living room. She gave one last, longing gaze, taking deep breaths as if she were trying to create a mental picture in her mind. She wanted to capture every detail of this moment. Bodel somehow felt that this would be the last time she would see him. He didn't ask for her contact details, and she didn't ask for his. However, there was a strange peace that rested in her heart. She looked at

Uncle Luis and Aunt Maddie with a loving sparkle that seemed to create a glow inside the entire room. She turned and walked up the stairs, glancing back once more to capture the look on her father's face before she retired to her room.